¡Mírame, ahí voy! / Watch Me Go!

MI MONOPATÍN RIPSTIK
MY RIPSTIK

Victor Blaine

Traducido por Eida de la Vega

PowerKiDS
press.

New York

Published in 2015 by The Rosen Publishing Group, Inc.
29 East 21st Street, New York, NY 10010

First Edition

Editor: Sarah Machajewski
Book Design: Mickey Harmon
Spanish Translation: Eida de la Vega

Photo Credits: Cover, p.1 (helmet) ronstik/Shutterstock.com; cover, pp. 1 (girl), 6 (wave boarding) Sergey Ryzhov/Shutterstock.com; pp. 5 (rider), 10, 18 bunebake/Shutterstock.com; p. 5 (helmet) Fred Sweet/Shutterstock.com; p. 6 (surfing) Logan Carter/Shutterstock.com; p. 9 © iStockphoto.com/Syldavia; p. 13 membio/Thinkstock.com; p. 14 http://en.wikipedia.org/wiki/Caster_board#mediaviewer/File:Wene-160-Skaten.JPG; p. 17 gorillaimages/Shutterstock.com; p. 21 Voyagerix/Shutterstock.com; p. 22 (boy) Digital Media Pro/Shutterstock.com; p. 22 (wave board) http://commons.wikimedia.org/wiki/Category:Caster_boards#mediaviewer/File:Waveboard_total_1.JPG.\.

Library of Congress Cataloging-in-Publication Data

Blaine, Victor.
My ripstik = Mi monopatín RipStik / by Victor Blaine.
p. cm. — (Watch me go! = ¡Mírame, ahí voy!)
Parallel title: ¡Mírame, ahí voy!.
In English and Spanish.
Includes index.
ISBN 978-1-4994-0282-7 (library binding)
1. Skateboarding — Juvenile literature. 2. Skateboarding — Technological innovations — Juvenile literature. I. Title.
GV859.8 B53 2015
796.6 —d23

Manufactured in the United States of America

CPSIA Compliance Information: Batch #CW15PK: For Further Information contact Rosen Publishing, New York, New York at 1-800-237-9932

CONTENIDO

- -

CONTENTS

Si quieres montar en algo fantástico, ¡monta en un RipStik!

If you ever want to ride something cool, try riding a RipStik!

6

Un RipStik es como un monopatín. ¡Montar en él es como hacer **surf** o snowboard!

A RipStik is like a skateboard. Riding one feels like you are **surfing** or snowboarding!

Al RipStik también se le llama tabla de olas. Los RipStiks y las tablas de olas son formas divertidas de hacer ejercicio.

A RipStik is also called a wave board. RipStiks and wave boards are fun ways to exercise.

Te paras en las **plataformas** del RipStik. Son lo suficientemente grandes para que te quepan los pies.

You stand on a RipStik's **decks**. The decks are big enough to fit your feet.

Cada plataforma tiene una rueda. Se controla una rueda con cada pie.

Each deck has one wheel. The rider controls one wheel with each foot.

Las plataformas están unidas por una barra. La barra hace que el RipStik se mueva.

The decks are joined by a bar. The bar helps the RipStik move.

Montar un RipStik puede ser difícil al principio. Puedes caerte. Usa un **casco** para evitar que te hagas daño.

Riding a RipStik can be hard at first. You may fall off. Wearing a **helmet** keeps you from getting hurt.

Después de que aprendas a montar RipStik, puedes aprender a hacer trucos.

After you learn how to ride a RipStik, you can learn to do tricks.

Hay un truco que se llama *kickflip*, es cuando haces girar la tabla en el aire.

One trick is called a kickflip. A kickflip is when you spin your board in the air.

¿Puedes hacer algún truco en tu RipStik?

Can you do any tricks on your RipStik?

PALABRAS QUE DEBES SABER / WORDS TO KNOW

(la) plataforma/
deck

(el) casco/
helmet

(el) surf/
surfing

ÍNDICE / INDEX

SITIOS DE INTERNET / WEBSITES

Due to the changing nature of Internet links, PowerKids Press has developed an online list of websites related to the subject of this book. This site is updated regularly. Please use this link to access the list: www.powerkidslinks.com/wmg/rips